JEASY

Hest, Amy.

The Friday nights of
Nana /
2001.

For my wonderful grandmother
A. H.

For Birdie, who showed me
that the beauty of the home is a wellspring of life
C. A. N.

Text copyright © 2001 by Amy Hest
Illustrations copyright © 2001 by Claire A. Nivola

First edition 2001

Library of Congress Cataloging-in-Publication Data

Hest, Amy.
The Friday nights of Nana / Amy Hest ; illustrated by Claire A. Nivola. — 1st ed.
p.   cm.
Summary: Jennie helps her grandmother prepare for a family Sabbath celebration.
ISBN 0-7636-0658-8
[1. Sabbath—Fiction. 2. Grandmothers—Fiction. 3. Jews—Fiction.]
I. Nivola, Claire A., ill. II. Title.
PZ7.H4375 Fr 2001
[E]—dc21   00-039784

2 4 6 8 10 9 7 5 3 1

Printed in Italy
This book was typeset in Centaur.
The illustrations were done in watercolor and pen and ink.

Candlewick Press
2067 Massachusetts Avenue
Cambridge, Massachusetts 02140

The Friday Nights of Nana

Amy Hest

illustrated by Claire A. Nivola

CANDLEWICK PRESS
CAMBRIDGE, MASSACHUSETTS

The Friday nights of Nana begin early Friday morning in her kitchen, and we are eating bread with sweet peach jam, which is her favorite and mine. Nana sips tea and the tea is too hot and she blows in the old china cup, making ripples.

"Today I have no school!" I sing. "Lucky me!"

"Today you have no school!" she answers. "Lucky ME!"

"Now tell about tonight," I say.

"The family is coming! The family is coming for Sabbath and we have work to do!" Nana zips inside to make the bed and tidy the rooms. I'm in charge of fluffing pillows.

Nana washes the good china and irons all the wrinkles
in her lace tablecloth. I fold napkins with lace borders.

She checks for missing buttons on her Sabbath dress,
navy blue with a round white collar and white cuffs, too.

"Is it time to make pie?" I ask.

"Soon, Jennie."

I polish, and polish, two candleholders.

"Now is it time?"

"Now," Nana says, rolling out dough, and I sweeten apples for the pie with sugar. Then she braids challah breads, and tucks them in the oven.

At noon we eat sandwiches in the park near the river.
There's cocoa, too, in teacups.

The sky is gray and wind blows off the river, blowing
our hair straight up, and we dance to keep warm, wearing
ponchos and mittens.

Afterward, we hold hands on city streets, looking for
violet-colored flowers, which are Nana's favorites and mine.
The flower man wraps them up in green wrapping paper.

"Why, thank you," says Nana.
And, "Thank you," I say, skipping along with my flowers.

When we get back to Nana's, we put them in a tall vase with water.

"Is it time to get dressed?" I ask.

"Soon, Jennie."

By late afternoon the house is all scrubbed, barley soup simmers, and the challahs cool off. Chicken is baking, and also the potatoes.

"Now is it time?"

"Now," Nana says, and we get dressed up in dresses that are both navy blue. Our shoes are blue, too. Nana puts on lipstick, watching her lips in the mirror.

We set the table, counting silver and soup bowls, glasses that sparkle. Nana pokes the chicken to see if it is tender.

Outside it is getting dark. "Look, Nana, snow!"

The doorbell rings and the family pours in, hugging
Nana. They hug me, too, especially my parents, and I
tickle my baby brother, Lewis, in his baby-bunny sleeper.

The doorbell rings and more family pours in! The
uncles, aunts, and cousins. Everyone talks at the same
time, kicking off boots, dropping coats on chairs.
You can smell my pie in the oven.

"Is it time?" I ask.

"Now," Nana says, and finally it's the best time.
Nana is lighting candles and our dresses are touching
and she is whispering Sabbath prayers and no one makes
a peep. Not even Lewis.

Soon we are munching the challahs and passing soup bowls, and everyone talks at the same time at the long dining table.

Outside, the wind howls. Snow whips up in great
white swirls.

But here inside, the candles flicker.
A Sabbath song is in the air. It's time for
pie and we're all here together on the
Friday nights of Nana.

❖ ❖